Henry and the White Wolf

BY **TYLER KARU** AND **TIM KARU**

WORKMAN PUBLISHING · NEW YORK

Library of Congress Cataloging-in-Publication Data
Karu, Tyler.
Henry & the White Wolf / by Tyler Karu & Tim Karu.
p. cm.
Summary: Henry, a very sick little hedgehog, receives treatment from
the White Wolf that makes him feel even worse but eventually cures him,
and through the ordeal he holds a stone to help him stay strong and brave.
ISBN 0-7611-2135-8
1. Youths' writings, American. [1. Cancer—Fiction. 2. Sick—Fiction.
3. Medical care—Fiction. 4. Hedgehogs—Fiction. 5. Wolves—Fiction. 6. Youths' writings.]
I. Karu, Tim. II. Title. III. Title: Henry and the White Wolf.
PZ7.K1515He 2000
[E]—dc21   00-040415

Workman books are available at special discounts when purchased
in bulk for premiums and sales promotions as well as for fund-raising
or educational use. Special editions can also be created to specification.
For details, contact the Special Sales Director at the address below.

Workman Publishing Company, Inc.
708 Broadway, New York, NY 10003-9555
www.workman.com

Manufactured in China

First printing October 2000
10 9 8 7 6 5 4 3 2 1

This book is dedicated to
Kristen Ann Carr,
Benjamin Kavaljian,
and Jane Ulmer.

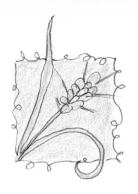

Once upon a time, not very far from where you live, in a hollow under a stone wall, there lived a hedgehog named Henry. Henry led a happy life in the forest and fields with his mother, Holly. Even though he was smaller than the other hedgehogs his age, Henry was much more daring. From the time he was just a baby, Holly taught her son the ways of the woods, and soon he had learned more than all the other little hedgehogs. He knew that the mouse would steal your food while you slept, and the squirrel would take it from right under your nose. He knew he must hide from men with dogs, and find shelter during thunderstorms. But most important, Henry knew that small animals should never go near the wolf's den.

One day while Henry was gathering food, he began to feel weak and dizzy. Henry got scared and dropped all the acorns he had found. He tried to walk back to the stone wall, but he just couldn't continue. So he found a safe place in the field and waited for his mother to find him.

Sure enough, Holly found Henry soon after he had gone to sleep. She tried to help him up, but he couldn't move.

So Holly gathered the softest grass she could find, and made Henry a snug bed in the field where he had waited. Then she asked her friend Sarah Spider to stay and watch over him.

"Don't move and stay very quiet," said Holly. "I must go find the Wise Owl."

And with that Holly scurried off as fast as she could. Soon she was at the old oak tree in the middle of the woods. This is where the owl sat and watched the hustle and bustle of the forest. Holly looked up at him with tears in her eyes.

"Wise Owl," cried Holly, "my son Henry is ill. He cannot move and is lying fast asleep in the field."

The owl looked down at her for a long time, then he looked left and right. Finally, in a voice both firm and gentle, he spoke.

"Go deep into the forest, and find the White Wolf. Only she knows how to cure your son."

"But Wise Owl," protested Holly, "everyone knows the rule of the woods: Never go near the wolf's den."

"Find the White Wolf," insisted the Owl. "Only she can help your son."

Holly turned and ran back to get Henry. She knew that he would have to walk to the wolf's den, and that it would be a difficult journey for him, but he could make it, for he was brave.

She found Henry lying in his bed of grass, fast asleep exactly as she had left him. Holly nudged him gently and woke him up.

"Henry, you and I are going to take a trip to the wolf's den."

"But Mother, everyone knows you mustn't go there," cried Henry.

"Just this once we are going to the wolf's den to find a way to get you better."

 So Holly and Henry made their way to the wolf's den. It was a slow journey, because Henry had a very difficult time walking. But Holly had faith in him and stayed by his side. Finally after a long day of traveling, mother and son reached their destination.

Holly saw the cave and was immediately stricken with fear. But not Henry. Even as sick as he was, the young hedgehog stepped right to the mouth of the cave.

"HELLOOOOOO?" called Henry, shocked at the way his voice echoed.

There was no answer. As he was about to turn back to his mother, a large pair of brown eyes appeared in the darkness. Henry looked into the cave and found himself face-to-face with a giant white wolf. The frightened hedgehog gasped at the size of the wolf, but tried not to show any fear.

"I'm sick," said Henry, almost in a whisper. "The Wise Owl said to find the White Wolf. I think I found you."

The wolf stared down at him with wide eyes. Slowly, a gentle smile crossed her pure white face.

"Yes, you certainly have," she said as she beckoned the two of them into her den. "The wolves here are healers, and we try to heal any creature who comes to us. You must understand, little one, that healing is not easy. Sometimes it is even very painful. You will probably lose all of your quills and soft fur, and you will feel very tired. The animals who know you now might look at you differently. But it is all for the best. No matter what, you must stay very brave and never give up."

"But I'm scared," whimpered Henry.

"It's normal to be afraid when you're sick, but you must always believe that you will get better. Your heart and your mind will help your body heal itself." The wolf's kind eyes lit up. She crossed to a shelf in the cave and picked up something Henry could not see.

"Take this and keep it with you while you are working to get well. It will always remind you that you are a strong, brave hedgehog," said the White Wolf solemnly. "Your strength and courage will help you get through the healing process."

Henry looked down and saw that she had placed before him a beautiful, rounded stone, perfect in size and smoothness. He picked it up and clutched it in his paw. Both Holly and Henry smiled as the White Wolf turned and led them farther into her den.

Deep in the darkness of the cave, the White Wolf gathered dried roots and berries and murky liquids and placed them in a small glass jar. Henry and Holly waited patiently while the wolf made an elixir for Henry.

Finally, the wolf placed a small bottle of ugly green potion on the table in front of Henry and Holly. Henry looked at it and frowned.

"I have to drink that, don't I?" asked Henry.

The wolf nodded. Henry stood up and hugged his mother, who looked even more dismayed than Henry. Holding his smooth stone tightly in his paw, Henry took the bottle from the wolf and drank the entire thing in one gulp.

Almost immediately he began to feel sick and dizzy. The potion tasted awful and Henry hated it.

"Now, you must both go stay in the hollow log outside the cave," said the wolf. "I will call for you when Henry must take the potion again."

Henry and Holly nodded, said thank you, and scurried out of the cave before the wolf could say anything else. For even though she was quiet and gentle, the White Wolf and her dark den made them both a little nervous.

 The two of them settled into the hollow log outside the cave. It wasn't very comfortable and they both would rather have been at home. Even so, they stayed. Every day the White Wolf would ask Henry to take some more of the potion. Each time Henry held the smooth stone in his paw, and gulped it down.

Soon Henry began to feel weak all the time. There were some days when he just couldn't get out of his bed. And just as the White Wolf had warned, he lost all of his beautiful fur and sharp quills. But one day, the wolf came to them and told Henry and Holly it was time for them to go home.

Henry made sure he had his stone with him. He wobbled up to the White Wolf, hugged her neck, and thanked her for her help. Then Henry and Holly began their long, slow journey back to their home in the field.

When they returned, Henry's friends were overjoyed to see him. They all gathered in the field to greet him. Henry smiled as he talked and laughed with his friends. It was a great day, and Henry was happy to be home.

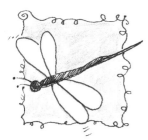But the next day was not so good for Henry. It was time for him to go back to school. Many weeks had passed since he had been there, and Henry was worried about what the other students would say to him. But he walked there on his own with the stone tucked securely in his paw. When he got to school, many of the animals did look at him differently. Some of them whispered, and Henry wondered what they were saying.

Henry's friend the mouse turned to him and asked, "Henry, why do you look different from all the other hedgehogs? Are you okay?"

Henry smiled at his friend's concern. Then he told him about getting sick, the White Wolf, and the gross green potion. All his classmates were amazed that Henry had actually dared to go into the White Wolf's den, and for days he was treated like a hero. They came to Henry over and over, asking him to tell them the story of the White Wolf.

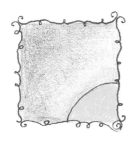 As the days became weeks, Henry felt better and better. His fur slowly grew back, and soon he looked just like all the other hedgehogs. On the day he was feeling the best, he heard a howl from beyond the hollow. He ran outside and found the White Wolf waiting for him. She looked down at him and smiled.

"Henry, I have been watching you for many days. I have seen you face your fears and stay brave. You are truly courageous, and best of all, you are healthy and strong once again."

Henry was so happy that he ran around the field twenty times before returning to thank the White Wolf.

"White Wolf, it is because of you that I am feeling so strong, and the stone you gave me has helped me conquer my fears. Whenever I hold it in my hand, I feel I can overcome any obstacle."

The White Wolf smiled at him, and before Henry could say anything more, she ran back into the woods.

The next night, Henry and his friends had a party. All of the creatures, including the White Wolf and the Wise Owl, were invited. Henry was the life of the party, and he was able to dance every dance.

And throughout the evening,

clutched in his paw,

was the perfect,

smooth stone.

THE TIMES I HAVE BEEN BRAVE

Henry always tried to stay brave and strong. This is your place to remember when you did the same. Fill in the lines below with some memories of your own bravery and strength. Refer back to them when you need a reminder of how courageous you are.

Michael
the white wolf

About the Authors

Tyler and Tim Karu are in high school in Portland, Maine, where Tyler pursues interests in art and community service. She will be entering college in Washington, D.C., in the autumn of 2000. Tim has recently finished his third screenplay and designs Web sites in his spare time. Tyler and Tim hope to collaborate on other books for children who are facing serious health problems.

TYLER

TIM

A Note from the Authors

What started out as an idea in the summer of 1998 has grown into a project that we hope will help sick children around the country. Writing this book has involved many people. Most of them are members of our family.

Our aunt, Stephanie Pilk, worked with us on the illustrations for the book.

Our other aunt, Roberta Pilk MacDonald, was instrumental in getting the book laid out and printed in its first incarnation.

Finally, our mother Candace Pilk Karu, helped with every aspect of *Henry & the White Wolf*. She was the driving force behind our work. This project would not have been possible without her.

We first learned about the Maine Children's Cancer Program in 1996. That year, our family worked on a project to raise money for MCCP. We toured their facilities and found out about the amazing work that goes on there. We also learned that kids being treated for cancer, especially the very young ones, can get really scared. Since we have both had our own experiences in hospitals, we wanted to do something to help kids stay strong and brave while going through the process of hospitalization or chemotherapy. This is why we wrote *Henry & the White Wolf*. We both know firsthand that hospital stays can be a frightening experience. This was just part of the inspiration for our story, but it is the one with which we can identify the most.

Thanks to all the people at Maine Children's Cancer Program who read and commented on our book, especially to Jim Bouchard, the Development Director at MCCP and Craig Hurwitz, the Medical Director.

If you have any questions about this project, please write to us care of Workman Publishing Company, 708 Broadway, New York, NY 10003 or e-mail us at Tntkaru@aol.com.